Clint Faraday
book fifty two
Killer Deal

Clint is in David for supplies. He will spend the night, then return to Quebrada Tula where he and his family are staying.

He is at Peter's Bar when he meets Sam Hires, who says he's made a killer deal for a fishing boat. He gets all the permits and such to do with it. It will run out of Mariato, which Clint knows.

Sam probably didn't mean "killer" deal the way it turned out.

Or did he?

Contents

About the author

CD Moulton has traveled extensively over much of the world both in the music business, where he was a rock guitarist, songwriter and arranger and in an import/export business. He has been everything from a bar owner to auto salvage (junkyard) manager, longshoreman to high steel worker, orchid grower to landscaper, tropical fish farmer to commercial fisherman. He started writing books in 1983 and has published more than 350 books as of January 1, 2023. His most popular books to date are about research with orchids, though much of his science fiction and fantasy work has proven popular. He wrote the CD Grimes, PI series, and the Det. Nick Storie series, Clint Faraday series, and many other works.

He now resides in Gualaca, Chiriqui, Panamá, where he writes books, plays music with friends, does research with orchids and medicinal plants. He has lately become involved in fighting for the rights of the indigenous people, who are among his closest friends, and in fighting the extreme corruption in the courts and police in Panamá.

He offers the free e-book, *Fading Paradise*, that explains what he has been through because of the corruption.

CD is the discoverer of the Chadam Protocol for curing cancer.

Facebook page Ambrosia peruviana for cancer.

Bar Talk

Clint Faraday, retired PI from Florida, in David, Chiriqui, Panamá, for supplies to take to his home in Quebrada Tula on the comarca Ngobe Bugle nodded to Jessie. She opened a Balboa and came to welcome him back.

"Same old crowd, I see," he said.

"Yeah. It doesn't change much. A lot of them, they're the same person with a different face. Same brags about things they don't have.

"I hear you just had your sixtieth birthday. You don't look that old."

"Seventieth, and thanks!"

"Oh. Here comes the only new one since you were here, but he's just another of the ones who have big plans that won't work.

"Sam Hires. He's going to run a fishing boat out of Mariato and make a million dollars the first month. I predict he won't last the first month.

"He's from New York originally, but ran a boat out of California . He knows hundreds of people ... you can hear it and get a laugh.

"Sam! Que tal? This is Clint. He knows the Mariato area. Maybe he can tell you about some of it."

"Not another one who's gonna tell me how I'll lose my ass I hope?"

"You already know it apparently. Why would I care?" Clint already knew he wasn't going to much like this one. His attitude was of the "I know everything and my mind's made up so don't try to confuse me with facts!" type.

"I know it's a killer deal! If there was ever a deal that can't miss, it's this one! I *know* this business! I ran a couple boats out of San Diego for this kind of thing. People would come from Europe to fish in my boats! Hell's fire! I know fifty people who'll be here as fast as I can get into operation! Three hundred a day per, run seven days a week, that boat, ten people. That's three grand a day, seven days a week. Twenty grand a week after expenses.

"I know how to find fish. I've already been out enough to know I'll never have a problem with that!

"I can advertise that you might see a pod of whales going by! I could do that in San Diego! Big draw!!

"So! Now tell me why I'm going to lose my ass!"

"This isn't San Diego, they aren't the same fish.

"Jessie, has German Jimmy come back from

Bavaria yet?"

"No," from Jessie.

"What do you mean? Not the same fish? A fish is a fish," from Hires. "Use the right bait, you catch them."

"Okay. Like I give a shit," Clint replied. "You might pull it off. Good luck."

"Just why do you think I'll fold here? Why does everyone here try to fight a guy trying to make a living? Why is everyone so negative?

"That's the thing that's different from the states! If you try to do anything like this there they give you encouragement! If there's a reason it won't work, they'll tell you! These people don't have a concept of business! They're totally ignorant about it. It's a matter of knowing the right people and getting the right reputation.

"You just don't know the business either. You lost your ass in some deal so now you want everyone else to come up a failure!"

"Clint's made millions of dollars," Jessie said. "I don't think you could call him a failure. He said right from the first that he didn't give a damn if you win or lose. It's *you* who won't drop it!"

"You want a few reasons?" Clint asked. "You got it!

"I take it your clients in San Diego were upper end level Europeans who came to California on a vacation and used your boat. You've obviously been to Mariato. How does a picturesque isolated fishing village compare to San Diego? Will any of those people come to a place where there's nothing but scenery for a hundred kilometers in any direction?

"That's just one of the things that occur to a person immediately."

Hires looked shocked. He turned his back and went out on the balcony. Jessie smirked at Clint and said, "Now's a great time to point that out!"

Clint laughed. "So he ran a boat in California and thinks it's the same here. Typical!"

"He didn't run any boat. He hires people for that. He sat in an office and booked the trips, an hour a day. He made twenty thousand a week – in California.

"He got a deal on a confiscated boat there. It's worth about a million and he got it for three hundred thousand. He found some letters on it that showed him the people who owned it came to Mariato several times a year and said the fishing was better than anywhere they'd ever been. He sold his California business and came here."

Clint looked thoughtful. "A drug runner who came to Mariato, an isolated fishing village, several time per year and reported on the great fishing, then the boat ends up getting confiscated in California.

"Doesn't sound too logical does it?"

"He's another one of those. He's going to make enough to buy Panamá the first year, then he's going to become the richest asshole in the world because we're all so ignorant.

"Then he goes home six months later dead broke."

Clint grinned. "Or something."

Clint was lounging on the cool front porch of his Quebrada Tula place. He had spent the day helping his people work with timber and had just come from the stream where he and his family had bathed. His daughter, Nicole, was helping his wife, Tyna, fix a sumptuous dinner. His son was in his room doing his homework

His cellular rang. It was satellite, so could be used here in the middle of the mountains.

"Clint Faraday? I'm Chico Vendres, police, in Mariato. Emilio Marcasa is a friend of yours?"

"Emilio? Yes. What's wrong?"

"He is alright. He suggested that I call you. There is a notice here that you are to be given every cooperation in legal matters. You were of great help with that land theft thing.

"There is a man here who has established a business with fishing boats. Very wealthy people come to use the service.That is acceptable. It offers some income to the area, though some of his clients are not the kind we welcome here.

"He has twice taken people out on the boat who didn't return. No mention was made of them.

"Beto, who takes information when they leave the port, says he recognized the one from today. He is a person who is suspected of many things. Emilio said you would know what to do so that we may discreetly seek information about what is going on.

"I take it you can determine that I do not like Mr. Hires, who runs the boat. I have some great suspicion of him. That boat was here many times a year ago and more. I was suspicious of what they were here for.

"The land thing in which you became involved was because a man was trying to set up a drug drop-off place. I have often thought his partners who were never caught have now finished that project, though I have been unable to confirm anything.

"I may, according to headquarters notices, send a helicopter to transport you here?"

Clint remembered talking to Hires three weeks ago about his "killer deal." He remembered what Jessie had said about the deal.

"Okay. I can be ready to go anytime, but it's getting dark now. The chopper can't find me at night. Anytime tomorrow will suit me."

"As early as the helicopter can take you aboard. At the dawnlight?"

"Good enough!"

Clint told Tyna and the kids he would be away again, but probably not for very long. It didn't seem to be the kind of thing that would take a lot of time. It was something he already had some ideas about.

He packed a few things in a backpack and would be ready when the chopper came. He was always up before there was enough light. This wouldn't be anything out of the ordinary.

The chopper came. He knew the pilot. They exchanged stories about what had happened to them since he last took Clint anywhere. It wasn't much and was a lot at the same time.

It was three hours to Mariato. There was little other than jungle below for much of the way.

The chopper sat in a field about a block from the police station. Chico was waiting. He took him to a little restaurant a short distance away where he had coffee and hojaldres while they talked. Most of what was said was about what Clint expected. Hires was not liked, but was tolerated because he did bring in some income to several people. Many of the people who used his services weren't liked anymore than him. They were the type you were more likely to fear than to respect.

Chico told Clint what he knew, then they went to the dock Hires used to talk with Beto Lopez, who kept track of everything going on there. He had a small fishing tackle shop at the base of the dock and furnished security when people left their boat there to go into the town, such as it was, or to got other places. The bus service was fairly dependable to the nearer points of interest.

It seemed that there was an unexpected flow of customers for Hires' fishing boat runs. The only problem was that only about a fourth of the people who used the service had any fishing equipment. Several of the customers were being watched discretely by the police. For various reasons.

That was also a sticking point. Various reasons. Only a couple because of drug trafficking.

"I know how to spot someone carrying drugs or a lot of money or whatever," Beto explained. "There's no evidence that is any part of it. I can't figure what *is* part of it!

"I wouldn't worry about it if there was some reason a certain group would hang together, but a lot of them are in different ... areas. We know that the Gomez group don't get along with the Cano group who don't get along with the Samosa group and so forth, but they all go out together. In two weeks I've seen people from those and other groups on that boat. It was a Samosa a couple of weeks ago who didn't come back, and a Gomez yesterday. The people who went out are the same people who came back in. They definitely aren't exchanging people out there.

"Gomez is too big to not be missed, and fast! I'm afraid there will be big trouble. I couldn't believe Samosa not coming back didn't cause a problem, but no one ever mentioned it."

"We checked with the people in Panamá City. He hasn't been seen since he came here. A man closed his house and said he was in Colombia, but we know definitely that he isn't there," Chico said. "This doesn't make sense to me."

They discussed everything they could, then Clint went to the station. Hires had left with a group about three quarters of an hour before Clint arrived. There were people from the Gomez group aboard plus several from the Cano group. The two groups did not like each other. They were both into construction fraud and such in a big way. They were bitter competitors.

"I'm afraid that what is going on out there is the groups are consolidating. If Gomez and Cano have an agreement Samosa can be forced out," Chico explained. "As it is they compete for bids and there is some saving to the people. If one group gets control of a large section things will get very nasty."

Clint agreed to see what he could learn. This didn't make much sense, but it was a dangerous situation for a lot of people who weren't involved in anything crooked. He would try to stop that!

This one, gossip and such would serve pretty well. For finding a starting place. Clint wished Judi was there. She could get information better and faster than anyone he'd ever known before.

He could talk with his Indio friends to learn something, possibly. They noted a lot of things, but didn't mention them. Too much of the so-called civilized cultures didn't make sense to them.

He found Benito and Santos at a little café having coffee, so joined them.

You don't beat around the bush with the Indios. If they feel you're hiding anything, you're just wasting your time trying.

"I need to know anything you might know about the boat. Hires."

Santos shook his head. "They are very strange and very dangerous people. They don't like each other. Any of them. It is all about money or power or something. They go because they will be the ones talked about if they don't."

"Yes," Nito agreed. "None of them trust any other of them even when they come together. Yesterday they almost carried one man onto the boat. He didn't want to go, but two others, bigger than him, took him onto the boat."

"That one didn't come back," Santos said in a warning tone. "He is probably feeding the crabs now. I think they killed him out there."

Pablo, another Indio who fished the near area, had just come to say "Hello!" to Clint. He added, "I was by the gate when they came in. He was with that big black with the gold chains and tattoos all over his arms They were laughing at something and getting the rods from their car and were going down toward the boat when the big limousine, the silver-grey one, drove in. The one who never came back saw them and started to argue with the black one. He said he was not going on any boat if Carlos Selasia was there!

"The black said something and a tall thin man in a suit came to them. They made him go on the boat."

Clint had heard of Carlos Selasia. He was a big distributor of illegal cigarettes. He was from Costa Rica. It was rumored he sold ninety five percent of the illegal tobacco supply coming into Panamá. He also sold rum and guns if the stories were true.

"That boat was here about a year ago?" Clint asked.

Nito nodded. "It came for more than two years. It would go to Puerto Armuelles and here, then to other places, then come back. I heard Jaime talking about Peru and Ecuador sometimes so I think they went there."

"My brother fishes out of Limones," Pablo said. "The boat would always go there before Puerto Armuelles. Always at night."

Clint knew Limones. It was on the narrow peninsula less than a kilometer across to Costa Rica. That would explain exactly one group that used the boat.

Two. Peru and Ecuador would be Cano. It wasn't drugs. What was it? For Cano, it wouldn't have anything to do with alcohol or cigarettes. For Selasia, it wouldn't be much else.

His big question: Regardless of what it was, why here?

<u>*A Weird Cast of Characters*</u>

Clint decided to accidentally meet Hires when he came in. Chico said he stayed in a rented place just past the town and ate most meals in the Cantina del Mar. The boat would be back about five if it followed the normal pattern.

This was something tied to various crime syndicates, it would seem. Clint called his friend, Manny Matthews (Who was actually Marko Bocinni, a very powerful mafia don who Clint had helped establish a new identity where he could escape his past. He still had vast power, people believing he was on a private island in the Mediterranean) to see if there was any word.

"I heard a little bit about some guy who was trying to consolidate a couple of the smaller groups into a kind of co-op. It's not likely, but I can check. If those people start working together, it could be very bad news for that whole area. Gimme a name?"

"Sam Hires, US. Gomez, Samosa, Martín and Eduardo Cano. Here, Costa Rica, Peru, Ecuador. Carlos Selasia."

Many whistled. "It's bigger than we thought.

Selasia's a pain in the ass. I don't know who the others are, but I will in an hour. Is Gomez the big construction bird who's getting all kinds of government contracts in Veraguas and Panamá Provinces?"

"Was. Julio Samosa was."

"Sounds like, 'Join us or join the fish!' to me."

"Me too."

"They fucking with anyone but each other yet?"

"Not that I know of."

"We can keep an eye on them for a day or two. I want to know something about that Hires person. I may have heard a little rumble about him in California. Bought a boat that certain people hadn't had time to remove a couple of things from. No problem – until he decided to sell his profitable business and go somewhere."

"He came here. What was in it? Something that gave him an in with those cruds?"

"The Bittermans were using it for a couple of years for running little specialty cargoes around various places. A cargo to San Diego was about fifty pounds of high grade processed coke. They weren't quite experienced enough to get it through, but they got their boat confiscated."

"I see. 'Oh! Dear god! I had no *idea* there was anything like that, blah, blah, blah!' line?"

"Uh-huh. I'll call in about an hour."

Clint went to the station to talk a bit more with Chico and to get some information about the boat and the people who ran it before. Chico gave him some sheets from the file to look over.

Lily's Little Pet, registered Panamá. 1998 54 ft' Engles-Craft, Insrd val. US$1,145,0 00.00. The registration was normal enough. The ports of call were pretty much what he already knew. There was nothing in that.

The last page was interesting:

Suspicious calling at ports not reported by captain. Between ports with facilities. Possible plus and possible minus.

Report: called on known drug processor Peru.

Report: 2 cases contraband tobacco confiscated – expln. was brought aboard by passenger, not to be offloaded Panamá.

Report: Called on known money laundering person Tabago.

The last entry was as interesting:

Confiscated San Diego, Calif. USA. Tip from no ID released local captain who saw transfer offshore.

Manny could find who that captain was in California in seconds! This might be a break – and might bring some facts to light that Hires would very certainly not want exposed!

Clint called Manny, who said he found

something very much off-kilter already.

"Clint, get out of there for now! I've arranged for you to get a flight from Santiago to San Diego. You'll meet Eddy Fellows when you get off the plane. He'll fill you in. I can't talk about it on the phone.

"It's a favor, but also for your case. It might not mean anything or it might mean a bunch of politicians in the states are going to pull another Ollie North scheme that could cause a few wars among cartels and could expand to a couple of countries being at each others' throats!

"I don't think the government's behind this one. Surely Obama's not that stupid!

"I might ask that you help some of my people in this. It's dangerous, Clint. I won't hold it against you for one second if you tell me to fuck off.

"Clint, your family's safe where they are. Mine isn't. There's something not right about this. It's coming from Southern California? I wasn't told about it?"

"I'm in. All the way!"

"I've asked that the chopper get you to Santiago. Fast! They'll hold the flight for as much as half an hour. It shouldn't be nearly that late."

Clint agreed to get to Santiago as fast as he could. He called Tyna and explained that he had to get to the states. He called Obilio, the comarca chief, to ask that no who's one not Ngobe be allowed within ten kilometers of his family. That was quickly agreed.

He went to the police station where Chico said arrangements had been made for Clint to go. No one was to know he wasn't working nearby for the police department. A very powerful man in the government had made it plain that there was to be no breach of security on that item. He didn't know what was going on – and didn't want to!

"To tell the truth, neither do I. If my friend gets this upset about it it has to be very big.

"Keep an eye on that boat and on Hires, but discrete."

"That is plain enough without the saying.

"Bien viaje and bueno suerte!"

Clint went to the hotel, grabbed what little he had there, swore because he didn't have his passport, so called Manny with that bit of news. Manny said he wasn't going to be him. There would be a passport waiting for him in Santiago. He was going to be "Charlie Brown" Furness, representative of Arturo Doniletti, of New York, doing a favor for a friend.

"Doniletti? Hasn't he gone legit?" Clint asked.

"Yes, but that doesn't mean he isn't still one of the most powerful men in the states. Anyone there will think it would be a very bad idea to cross either of us if we're such good friends.

"True, so you're solid with that."

"I'm on my way. I hear the chopper coming in."

California Dreamin'

Clint got off the 707 dead tired. He'd just made it to Santiago and had rushed aboard. Manny had somehow made the arrangements where his passport was stamped and he was in flight in less than five minutes. The people at the airport seemed to be in awe of him. He wondered what the story was.

There was a big man with a pony tail and too much flashy jewelry standing by the arrival door with a sign that said, "Charlie Brown" in big letters. Clint went to him and asked if he was Eddy Grant.

"No. Eddy Fellows. Your name really Charlie Brown? Like in the comics?"

"No. What's the skinny?"

"We'll get your bags and I'll fill you in."

"This is it." Clint held up the little maleta with one change of clothes and some extra underwear and shaving kit, etc.

"You came all the way from Detroit with just that?!"

"Hell, no! New York! I travel light. I don't want to have to hang around here a month."

They went out and got in a showroom powder blue '67 GTO. Traffic was ridiculous. Clint was glad, again, that he was out of that rat race.

"I'm supposed to be introduced to some people who know things they aren't talking about. I'm working this time for your boss. Seeing Artie is also in it maybe they'll loosen up, huh?"

"Shee! You call him Artie? Doniletti? Isn't it always Mr. Doniletti, SIR!?"

"I call him Artie, he calls me Fuckhead. My Pops and him lived close and did a lot of things together. I knew him all my life."

"You ever meet Mr. Bocinni?"

"I knew Joe and I know Marko."

"I never met Papa. They say he was a real trip."

"Yeah. Sicily all the way, but a big heart in some ways. You meet him out somewhere, he's just this real character old Italian guy."

"Well, I'm going to introduce you to a guy who works at the marina. Has for fifteen years. Knows a lot of shit, don't say nothing. He knows too much about a lot of people. You get your ass in a real crack if you pressure him. Just a warning.

"You know what it's about?"

"Not really. Marko has some friend in a place south of here who's about to get involved with a bunch of amateur clowns who'll just fuck up the business for a lot of people. Marko wants the problem stopped before it gets to be a problem.

"What I hear, it's a group who'll try to move in here and in the other side of the country. It's for him and Artie ... and Mo and Greco, too. Even DeGuilio might be brought into it. That's something that they do *not* want to happen, ever, for any reason." Clint was trying to remember what two detectives from Florida had told him when they happened to meet him in David. Pancho DeGulio was a shadowy character who had every mobster in the states and several other countries terrified of him, not because of anything he'd done, but because of what he knew. He was behind Doniletti, Greco and Mo going legit.

"DeGulio?! My god! I have to ... really?"

"Yeah. Marko and Artie both say this shit has to stop. Here and now!"

"I reckon!"

They pulled up in front of a huge hotel. Eddy took him in and said there was a room waiting for him. He'd be back in an hour or so to take him to the marina.

He went in to the desk to get his room, saw that it was in front, and asked that they transfer him to a room in back where it was quieter. They did.

He didn't doubt there were a half dozen bugs in the room they had for him. He didn't mean cockroaches.

When he was in the room he took out the new cellular Manny had waiting for him at the airport and called him.

"Manny, I'm getting a number of very strange reactions from your man, Eddy."

"Example?"

"I said DeGulio might become involved. He almost shit. He said he had to...."

"What?"

"He didn't finish the sentence."

"I see."

"Wasn't I supposed to go directly to the marina with him?"

"Where are you?"

"In the hotel. He'll pick me up in an hour or so."

"I don't need to ask if you changed the room. Maybe it would be best if you just came back here before they set something up. I actually will contact Artie. I know he and DeGulio get along. If DeGulio says he would be ever so slightly interested in knowing about a boat and some crud named Hires you could fill a library with what he would get in ten minutes.

"I wonder if I really could get in touch with him. I wonder if I have the balls!"

"I can get in touch with him. Nick is a very close friend. He'd do that for me."

"Maybe alert your friend about it? Don't do

anything now."

"I think I will. I'll talk to him. I won't mention you."

"I don't know what to suggest now. It might be better if you don't go anywhere with Eddy. It sounds like he's playing both ends. That would mean they have a story for you."

"I'll feel my way. I might even tell Eddy-boy that Mr. DeGulio, Your Majesty, said not to listen to any shit from the group, that he might take a personal interest in it."

"Clint! Stop it! Don't go off half-cocked! Not where DeGulio is concerned! Please!"

"I'll take the greatest care. Promise."

They chatted for another few minutes, then Clint looked up a number and called it.

"Hello?"

"Janet? Clint Faraday here. Is Nick around?"

"Oh! Clint! I'm still not over that visit! Are you in paradise right now?"

"No. I'm in hell. Called California."

"Well, Nick's at work. Anything I can do? You can call him at the station."

"No. I want to get in touch with Mr. DeGulio. Something very sinister is going on that includes Doniletti and Bocinni as well as Panamá and points north and south."

"Pancho? I'll call him. Stay on the line. I'll

conference it.”

He waited, then Janet Storie said, “Pancho, this is Clint. I told you about him. He needs a favor or something. I know you can trust him.”

“Yes. I know. Dave told me about him and the things he’s doing and that Marko Bocinni is a friend.

“Mr. Faraday, what can I do for you?”

“It’s Clint, Mr. DeGulio. I think something is up that could cause no end of problems for a lot of people in a lot of places. Does the name Sam Hires mean anything to you?”

“I’m Pancho. Any friend of Nick and Janet – and Dave – is a friend of mine.

“Hires. I think ... a moment. I’ll bring it up.

“San Diego?”

“Was. Now, Mariato, Panamá.”

“Hmm. What’s he up to? Should Jan know about it?”

“No. It wouldn’t be safe.”

“Jan, please drop out. I’ll tell you and Nick anything I can.”

“Okay. I don’t want to know from nothin’! Ciao!” She dropped off.

“Give, Clint. Is Bocinni involved?”

“Yeah. I think all of them from Doniletti to, who was it? Greco? And some character named Mo.

“I think Hires is trying to set up some kind of co-op or something among all the bigger crime people here and in South America. I can't see what else it could be. He's running a fishing boat he got at auction. It was seized for running drugs. Bitterman. He found something on that boat and has been in contact with the whole lot. Two that I know of went out on that boat and didn't come back. Gomez and Samosa."

"There are rumors. The Canos involved?"

"Definitely. He was on the boat when Samosa disappeared. Also Selasia."

"Carlos Selasia?"

"Yes."

"You are in California. Tell me why."

Clint explained what had happened so far.

"They will make up a story. They have to get that person at the marina in on it. You are in some danger. You will call this number when you are all together. I will try to make them pause to consider possible consequences by the mere fact you are reporting to me. I am raising a family here in Florida, as Marko is on Isla San Cristóbal. I will try to not become involved, but this could be a very bad thing. We can work together to determine exactly what is planned and to thwart their plans. Dave says you are capable of thinking well on your feet. I will wait until you give me a direction when you call. I will have arranged to conference with Artie and others, should that prove advisable."

"Thanks, Pancho. Ask Nick about my places on the comarca. It's paradise. I think you'd like the area. I know I would like for you and your family to visit."

"I am from Peru. I know the paradise some of the places there can be. Perhaps I will someday come to visit you there. Dave has invited me as well. I think I would like a place such as he describes. Nick and Jan were very impressed to the point they are semi-seriously thinking of moving there someday.

"Tell Marko that there are some very ominous things happening in California. I believe there will be a big power play. Perhaps this is part of that. We will have to see it doesn't happen."

"I'll agree with that a hundred ten percent!"

The house phone rang. Clint said he enjoyed talking with Pancho and would probably call again within the hour. He answered the phone to have Eddy tell him he was ready to take him to the marina. He said he'd be right down.

They were soon headed for the marina. Eddy seemed a bit nervous. Clint asked why.

"Why did you change rooms?"

"I'm always with Artie and friends? I'm going to stay in a room someone else has ready?"

He didn't reply. They came to the marina and got out. Clint was taken to an office where he was introduced to Johnny Parks. There were two others in the office. Neither one looked like someone you would want to meet in a dark alley.

"Uh, this is Johnny Parks. He's sort of a dock manager. This is Hugo Smith and Edward Jones. Charlie Brown," Eddy introduced. They each grunted. Clint returned the grunts.

Parks studied Clint for a moment, then said, "Charlie Brown. Who is here for Arturo Doniletti at request of Marko Bocinni."

Clint shrugged.

"How come nobody around Doniletti ever heard of you, Charlie-boy?

"You should be more careful with the names you throw around!"

"Then Eddy, here, can tell you it wasn't Marko personally who told him to meet me here."

"I just got a message that *said* it was from him!" Eddy cried.

"Marko's living on a private island in the Mediterranean Sea. I've been there," Parks said, haughtily.

"Part time," Clint replied. "He's also got a little thirty room villa in Southern Spain. You've never been to either place. I'd strongly advise *you* about throwing names around."

"Yes? And you know Mr. DeGulio? Of all the names in the world, that's one you *don't* throw around! Ever!

"Bocinni is a has-been. He's not even around anymore. Doniletti is on the other side of the country."

"Not if you can't back it up," Clint agreed. He took out his phone. The two goons tensed. He smirked at them and punched the number.

"Yes? Charles?"

"This is on speaker, Pancho. Yes, they have a mole at Artie's. They got the report that I'd never been there."

"I see. I was speaking with Artie and Mo a few moments ago. I promised to find that bit of information for him. I also spoke with Marko, for which he's not exactly thrilled. It's the wee hours there. He will find it interesting that the person who took you to find some minor information has taken the steps he has taken.

"I'm on speaker? Very well.

"To the lot of you. I am becoming displeased at your duplicity. Should you not deal with Charles honestly and quickly I will find it necessary to express my displeasure.

"A moment. I have a call."

There was a long moment's silence, a very uncomfortable one for everyone but Clint, then

Pancho came back on. "I am in conference with Greco Miklokaras, Mo Jefferson and Artie Doniletti. I will patch you in. I have also tried ... here is also Marko Bocinni.

"Shall we continue? Charlie, what questions do you wish answered? Marko? Artie? Greco? Mo?"

"I would like to ask Eddy-baby what the fuck he thinks he's doing," Manny snarled. "I don't think I'm happy about this shit. At all!"

Eddy was staring at the phone in horror. "Mr. Bocinni! They forced me to tell them about it! I don't even know what's happening! Honest!"

"Yeah, right! I was there you'd be cut bait next fishin' trip. Can't trust nobody no more. Half-assed wimps without a clue. Shit! You sold out. Keep a lookout over your shoulder, turkey! One time soon there'll be somethin' there!"

"Yo, Artie! There's a mole at home," Clint said.

"Yeah. I know about Franko. He's like Eddy-boy there. I learn a lot by playin' stupid."

"What's the deal? A co-op?" Clint asked Parks.

"Look! It's not my idea! I told them it can't work. The families have run things for a long time and have this stuff figured in ten years before it happens! All I did was sell a boat at federal auction! Hires found some papers and started talking like a crazy man! He was going to become the most powerful person in the world by consolidating all the syndicates in Central and South America, then taking over here, then the rest of the world. He's crazy!"

"He would have every one of them gunning for him in a month," Pancho said. "To do something this stupid means he wouldn't have the brains to hold it together.

"Edward, take Charlie back to the hotel for his things, then to the airport. I've arranged for him to return home. I will intercede with Marko to please allow you to go. You have proven valuable to me. Do not again ally yourself with any group such as these.

"Parks, you will speak not one word of this to anyone. That is for all of you. By anyone, I mean anyone.

"Is that all for now?"

"Except that Parks should be warned about saying he's been to the has-been Marko's place in the Med," Clint answered. "His attitude says he's in this 'way over his head. Artie, you're on the other side of the country and can't do anything.

"This is just to let you know the act they're pulling here is bullshit. It's one hell of a lot deeper than this. Eddy and Eddy and Hugo are just everyday hoods. Parks is obviously running things here. Hires isn't here, which tells us a lot about who gives the orders. He claims to know where

Marko is. He said he'd been there, which everyone in town knows is bullshit."

"He's that stupid? Does he not realize that the
three others there will report that he said such
things? Does he not understand that there are a
number of very dangerous people who will kill
him to learn that location?

"Edward, did he tell you that falsehood before
this meeting?"

"No, Mr. DeGulio, Sir. I would know it was
bullsh ... a lie. Mr. Bocinni wouldn't allow such as
him to slop the hogs on one of his places. He took
me in, but Charlie Brown is right. He gives all the
orders, but doesn't check first. When I told him
about Mr. DeGulio he didn't make a call or
anything. He just said this is what we'll do. No
shithead like Charlie Brown would ever be in the
same building as Mr. DeGulio."

"We will, then, adjourn this meeting. Back
home, Charlie! Work to do.

"Don't anyone forget that this meeting never
took place. Not a word is to ever be let out. That
would anger me.

"Mr. Parks, you are one word from angering me
and two from enraging me. I hope that is clear."

He rang off. Everyone fidgeted and looked
miserably uncomfortable. Clint told Eddy he
wanted to get on that plane and get the hell away

from California. He almost said "The states," but caught himself.

He left. The three still in the room were looking sick and scared.

Maybe critically ill and terrified was more like it. Parks was pale and sweating in the cold air-conditioned office. He was incapable of saying anything.

Clint called Pancho as soon as he was alone to thank him. He asked if there was really a ticket waiting for him at the airport. Pancho said that was a matter of punching a few buttons on a computer.

"But, wouldn't the flights be filled this time of year anyhow?"

"I imagine so. It helps that I am a majority stockholder in the airlines,"

He called Jan and thanked her. Nick was home, so they chatted a bit on the ride to the airport. Eddy thanked him for keeping Marko from having him killed. Clint said Pancho did that, not him. He wouldn't dare make a suggestion to Pancho, even though they were friends.

"Those people want to be the most powerful in the world, or that Hires asshole and Parks. Mr. DeGulio *is*!" Eddy whined.

"I've heard that. He's really a very nice person. He cares about people. He doesn't want to be powerful. He wants to be left alone. That's why he gets along with Marko, I suppose. Marko looked around and asked what it was for. There's no reasonable answer to that question."

"I'd like a million or two. I can think of things to do with it!"

"You'd buy a lot of stuff you don't want and that would turn out to be something other than you thought."

"I don't know. I'd still like to try it. You ever handle a load of cash for them?"

"Not for them. I have a few million of my own. I know what I'm talking about."

"You got a few million and you do things like this for them? I don't get it!"

"They're friends, or Marko and Pancho are. I get along with the others very well. They know I'm the type who doesn't give a shit about what they do so long as they leave the innocent Joe out and, most important, never mess with a friend of mine."

"Except Mr. DeGulio! I'll bet you wouldn't go against *him*!"

"Pancho and I are a lot alike about that. There'll never be any reason to go against him."

"I could be a buddy with someone like you. You don't give any shit, you don't take any shit.

"Listen. Tell Marko that I really didn't have a

choice at first. After it looked like they would get a lot of money before Marko stepped on them, so I decided to try to get some of it. I would have told him about it as soon as they had the money together. Hires is setting it up so that they each give him a couple million to get in the group. A couple mil is nothing at all to them.

"Honest! I was going to tell Marko!"

"I'll tell him, but you'll keep trying to play both ends against the middle. You probably *will* end up cut bait if you don't wise up."

They got to the airport to learn Clint had twenty minutes before the flight left. Eddy asked why it was on that airline. It went to South America!

"With a stop in Mexico City where Charlie Brown will get off and Sam Spade will take the next flight to The Apple. That's why Artie's boy said I was never there." Clint improvised.

"Hey! That's cool! What's your real name ... oh, sorry."

"James Brown. That's why I'll never use that one."

Clint flew out on the flight.

Mariato was beautiful and tranquil after San Diego. Clint hadn't been able to get any sleep on the flight and was really beyond tired now. He went to the hotel, showered and as much as passed out. It was late, almost three AM. He didn't wake up until ten to nine, ridiculously late for him.

He called Tyna and spoke with her. Things were normal there. Alma Grimes was coming for a month to look for orchids with Dave. They were going to be in the southern and eastern Darien.

He ate a good breakfast and went to the police station. Chico said Hires was out with another group of fishermen today.

"Hires was asking about you. He said a friend saw you here. He met you in David. Beto told him you come here every once in awhile to visit friends or to help the police if we ask. You did catch a big wannabe gangster type who was trying to set up a drug drop-off here.

"He said he'd probably run across you if you stay around.

"What is he doing here?"

"Trying to set up a major control of all the drug

cartels and crime syndicates in Central and South America, basically. He has a plan to be able to control it all. I think the ones who tell him to fuck off are the ones who don't come back."

"There was a man by the name of Benicio Gomez here. He was talking with the Indios. Perhaps they will tell you what he wanted."

Clint nodded. They would tell him when they wouldn't talk to the police. He checked over his report, put it in the files and went to the dock. Santos and Pablo were there. He bought them coffee and chicha and asked if they would tell him about Benicio Gomez.

"His brother came to a meeting here and was supposed to go back to Medellin. He didn't go back yet. He said it was just a business meeting with Sr. Selasia and some gringo. Sr. Selasio sent a car for him and had a secretary to help him if he needed it. They were going to mix the business meeting with fishing because his brother liked to fish," Pablo answered.

"Gomez was one who went out, but didn't come back," Clint said. "This could mean trouble for Selasia and Hires, I would tend to think. They're dangerous people. Don't get involved with them in any way. They are criminals."

"We know Selasia is. We told them that we don't take people fishing. He would have to talk to Mr.

Hires. He did," Santos replied.

They chatted a bit about other things, then Clint went to the hotel, thought about the fact Hires knew he was there and went to a little stream to sit on the bank and make a few phone calls.

"Marko, Gomez has a brother who asked some friends about the fishing trip. It seems Gomez was supposed to go fishing with Selasia and never came back. Selasia is using his clout to get them together it seems."

"I was afraid of that. Selasia is a pain in the ass. He thinks he's about ten times as powerful as he is. I'll get some Colombian friends to explain the inadvisability of continuing on his present course. Watch your back around him!"

"Around any of them. Hires was asking about me so he knows I'm here. I guess Parks will get word to him some way."

"Fifty-fifty. If DeGulio says not to mention it to anyone there aren't many who would take the chance.

"I've got some business associates in San Diego checking on everything about Parks and Hires. Julia Bocci says she's had a run-in with him where he came out second best in a two horse race. She's legit now. She's a friend of DeGulio. They might handle that end in a way we'll never hear about it. She has connections, same as me."

They chatted about mundane things, then Clint called Pancho and explained what was going on. Pancho said he had someone watching all of them.

"Nick Storie, who you know, got into a little international intrigue a couple of times. He is a very practical sort, as you seem to be. He is aware that it is sometimes best for all concerned that those people settle their differences in their own way. Dave tells me you are also of that bent. You won't become involved unless your friends or innocent people are drawn into it.

"If Gomez were to learn that his brother was killed by those people I think he will have enough savvy to arrange something.

"I have found to this point that Selasia is using Hires and Parks. He wishes to become the don of all the Americas. He's an idiot, but smarter than Hires and Parks, who are naive enough to think they can take over.

"None of it would work, but it could start a war among the criminal elements on both American continents. A large number of people with no concern in it whatever could be harmed.

"We must see that doesn't happen."

"There we're in total agreement. I can see that Gomez and anyone in the Samosa group learn what happened to their bosses. I have the perfect person to get that done clear across the country! In

Bocas!"

"Ah! Judi! Dave has told me of her expertise at getting things done. If you aren't successful, I will employ cruder and more violent methods. I will try to keep it out of involvement with the people there."

"I'll be in touch!"

Clint soon called Judi Lum, his next door neighbor in Bocas Town, to ask her to help. There was no one who was better at that kind of thing. She would stay out of it very skillfully while causing what they wanted known to be known. She would arrange to get out of town with a story that there is a rumor that some big mafia boss from California was trying to con a few local wannabes into a co-op that he would use to make a deal for his own ass with DEA and the IRS, back in the states. Just a rumor. Those things *do* happen sometimes. You have to know if the CIA and FBI are in it it'll be so screwed up nobody will ever unravel it in our lifetimes!

He then called Tyna again. He was missing her and his family. He felt he was close enough to being over the need to run around the country with the detective work that he could be happy on the comarca.

He then went visiting. He knew some people in the area. He could get a better feel of how people were reacting to this situation. Most of them were simply staying out of it. That was the smartest approach. Let that bunch of violent thugs kill each other off!

Judi came in on the five o'clock bus. She had met the chopper Clint sent and been delivered to Tibario. She flagged the Mariato bus there and here she was.

Clint quickly explained what he needed. She found a room in the house of a friend of a friend and managed to be in the little café near the dock when Hires and Company came in at ten to six. She had a transmitter built into a lipstick tube in a mesh purse that she had casually dropped onto the table when she sat to order pineapple chicha and a cheese empanada.

Two men and a woman came from the boat to order hot coffee and chicken emparedadas. There were only three tables in the little café. Judi was in the center one. She could hear everything close. The transmitter could catch things she couldn't.

Judi managed to order another empanada in a badly accented Spanish, then try again in a worse accented English. Ana, the woman who ran the café, was in on it and told her to point to what she wanted on the menu sheet.

The woman asked her, in English, "Are you new here?"

"Taiwan from China, thank you very," Judi answered.

"Esta tourista?" a man asked.

"She," Judi answered.

They wished her a pleasant stay and started into a somewhat animated conversation. She was the only person who could possibly hear them, she didn't speak Spanish or English, the two languages they used. "Comacho" was discussed. He had gone out with them, but didn't come back.

Clint was listening to it through the transmitter. That was number four (?) and was probably a huge mistake, seeing their contact in California was suddenly out of it because of a heart attack.

Clint called Pancho. Park had a small heart attack and was using it as an excuse to become incommunicado. Clint said he overheard that today's disappearance was the fourth, and that they felt it was a big mistake.

"I had heard that a man, Sergio Ivaniez, was the first. He was before Hires started the boat service. Mexico. Today's would be ... they are noted ... Jorge Periniez. He went out. I haven't the report about ... yes. It's here on the computer. Raul Camacho?

"I figured that one wrong, but it was one or the other. I thought Camacho was stronger. He deals in legal things. Auto parts. It's the way they're obtained that isn't legal. Venezuela.

"It really was a mistake! He was the only one from Venezuela who they could reach, so that's out now.

"Perhaps you may discover why he was the one they got rid of?"

"Judi is listening to them right now. She has the transmitter you had Chico give me."

"I hope she has sense enough not to get too close? They will speak English there, I imagine. You can get what you want through the device.

"Clint! Inez Marinera is the woman on that trip! She will know about the transmitter! She has used similar, if not as sophisticated. I trust it is out of sight?"

"I'll call her now. How can she make it seem innocent?"

"Inez won't ... she doesn't know it can be miniaturized enough that real lipstick can be in the tube. Can your operative contrive to use the lipstick where she can be seen?"

"Judi can contrive anything! Later!"

He rang off and called Judi's cell phone. He said Inez would know that transmitter if it could be seen

"It's in a mesh bag. I think she could see it if she looked for it specifically."

"She doesn't know real lipstick can be in the

tube?"

"I'll handle it."

Judi took the last bite of her empanada and took out her compact to use a napkin to wipe off her lips. She frowned and fumbled around the mesh bag, brought out the lipstick, applied it, dropped the transmitter back into the bag and used the napkin to press the excess color off her lips. She noticed Inez having a startled look on her face when she took the tube out, then how she relaxed when she saw it was actually lipstick in the tube.

She looked at her watch, drummed her fingers on the table, then called Ana over and said she wanted a coffee with cream and a tiny bit of cinnamon.

"Café con crema con que?" Ana asked.

"Poquitita la canela," Inez said and smiled at Judi, who said, "Thank you very, I am sure!" brightly.

"You are welcome. It can be very difficult to converse when you have an imperfect grasp of the language," Inez said in the local Chinese dialect. Judi spoke it, but said, in the dialect of Taiwan, "It is good to hear a language I can understand much of, though the dialect here is more the trade dialect. I can manage it! Thank you for your kind help."

"I have some business with a number of the Chinese people here. I have learned some of the dialect. I hope you enjoy your stay here."

"It is nice. The people, such as yourself, are very good and considerate people in many ways."

The three left fairly soon. Judi finished her coffee with cream and cinnamon, which she didn't much care for, and went out.

Clint sighed and listened to the recording from Judi's transmitter. He selected several things and isolated them, then sent them to Pancho and Marko on the computer. He noted that Inez said Judi looked like a picture she'd seen in the newspaper. Some woman who was working with a famous detective building hospitals. Carlos should check her out. The problem was that the Chinese looked so much alike, but Judi was much more attractive than most of them so was more easily remembered.

Judi said she heard that. A man was hanging around the park when she went through two minutes ago. He was following her. She had the pepper spray ready.

Clint bolted for the door. He was near the park and got there just as Judi came toward the hotel. A man was just coming up to her. He said something and she turned to reply. He talked for a few seconds, then went on. Two musicians from Peru, very good with the Pan Pipes, were coming across toward her. Clint had seen them around the docks a few times.

Pancho had someone keeping an eye on the boat crowd. Pancho was from Peru.

Clint grinned. If what he'd heard about DeGulio was true, anyone who acted like they might someday even consider hurting Judi would be, as charged several times, cut bait – within minutes.

Clint waved for Judi to come into the hotel. He didn't want to be seen talking to her. The man and the musicians passed on.

"What?" he demanded when she was inside.

"He called for Miss Lum. I didn't turn around and he came to ask me if I was the Judi Lum on the television."

"What did you say?"

"I said, 'Oh! Hello and hi there! Please to call me Mimi! I speak only a little Spanish not very well much. Is to Judi a question?'

"He said he thought I looked like a Judi Lum who was on television with some detective.

"I said, 'Oh! Right and yes, please! My good friend sister of her I am! Mimi Whang. Very pleased meeting to you! What is your name?'

"He said he was Carlos. Welcome to Panamá!"

Clint immediately called Chico about that, and

Marko. They would be ready if any questions were asked. Pancho had warned them that Selasia was with this group.

Pancho called a few minutes later and said he'd learned that Judi was telling people she was her sister or the friend of her sister, thank you very. Clint said he'd told them that Judi was fast on her feet.

"And thanks for having those two nearby. Judi can handle herself, but these are professional killers."

"You spotted my men? How?"

"I knew you had someone here. You are from Peru. There are two musicians from Peru passing through."

"They have done nothing to draw anyone's attention?"

"A lot! They're superb musicians and will play a number for anyone for a dollar! Pink Floyd!"

Pancho laughed. "Well, I think this is coming down to the line. Hires is trying to contact Parks right at this moment. I wonder how Parks will handle it. I'm going to try to throw suspicion around that gaggle of clowns in all directions. Let's see how long their little alliance holds together, particularly now that they've killed a few of the opposition and don't have the solidity of protection they thought they had.

"Don't interfere, Clint. Let them rid the world of each other. It won't get past the group after this. They're going to feel they're more on their own that ever before. They know they can't be trusted, much less someone from outside!"

"Interfere?! Me! I have to warn them that they might be at risk from their own partners! This is terrible! Those lovely people might even go to the extreme of *killing* each other!"

"If we're lucky. I'll speak with you later. Be careful that you don't say anything that might warn them about what they are."

"Po l'il ol' innercent *me*?!"

"Caio!"

"Hasta lluego, Baby!"

Clint thought and giggled. He might actually be able to do something to make them go for each others' throats! It was worth the old college try!

He called Judi and said to accidentally meet him at the restaurant at eight. Maybe they could get this done fairly quickly. It was unraveling.

It was a little after seven. He cleaned up and dressed as much as he did, then headed for the restaurant.

Clint went into the restaurant and stood looking around. There were three people sitting with Hires at a table to the side. One woman, two men.

Judi came in from the restroom and saw him by the entrance. She cried, "Clint! Woo-hoo! Clint!" Hires and friends looked up. Judi ran to hug Clint and say her sister or friend of her sister or somebody said he was there in Mariato and she came to hope she might somehow see him again before the end of the world or sunset or tomorrow or something. She managed to mangle her English enough to where Clint had a little trouble not giggling.

"Oh? Judi went to Panamá City I hear. I know she wanted to show you around, but it was business with the hospital we're building in the comarca."

"She! Yes and all that and to where did I find you after all don't you see!"

"Er, yes. I'm here to visit Santos and Pablo, friends."

"Yes and too many don't the friends like you and how is Tyna or somebody in your son and daughter family?”

“Fine.”

“Uh! Judi say you to tell me about some big bad people with FBI and CIA or somebody else like that who isn’t where or anywhere to not know if true.”

“The FBI? I don’t know what ... I wish I knew some Chinese!”

When Judi mentioned the CIA and FBI the four at the table gave each other very strong looks. Inez came over to say, “You’re Mimi? We met earlier. Speak Chinese and I will translate for you.”

Judi said a few sentences. Inez translated, “She says the people on the boat are working for the CIA or FBI, but it is a rumor and only one or maybe two of them.”

She asked Judi something. Judi replied.

“She says – I’m sorry if I don’t get it exact. We speak a slightly different Chinese dialect – She says that the man on the boat from the United States who is supposed to be working for the mafia is really working for the FBI. It is only a rumor.”

She chattered at Judi, then staggered when Judi said something about DeGulio.

“Dios mio! I mean, she has mentioned a name that is terrifying to many people. If what she says is true there is very hard thing that must be faced."

"I heard her say DeGulio," Clint said. "Does she mean Pancho? Why hasn't he said anything to me? We talked just last week."

"You know DeGulio?!?"

"Well, Julia Bocci, I think it was, introduced me to him in Florida. She's from California, and was there with Artie Doniletti for his wedding. I was invited, which was a great honor. We agree on a lot of things. We're sort of friends.

"Ask her what Judi said. I'm not sure who she's talking about."

Clint had exceptional peripheral vision. He had never looked directly at the table. Hires came over to say, "Clint Faraday? We met in David?"

Clint turned and looked at him. "Oh, yes. Going to set the world on fire with a fishing boat. Mariato. So you actually did come ... Mimi? What boat? Did she say?"

Inez gave Hires a scorching look and chattered with Judi. Hires just looked uncomfortable.

"She says the boat from California that Marko said was supposed to be setting up another of those impossible syndicate co-op deals. There's a rumor the person in California and one of the people here, or maybe two or three, are working for the FBI and DEA through the CIA to get their own asses out of a serious long-term crack! They go away for life without if they don't cooperate."

"Shit! Why do those things always come to Panamá where I get involved? I couldn't care less what that bunch of clowns are doing. I certainly don't want anymore to do with the big bad CIA!

"Mimi, tell Judi ... never mind. I'll call her. Right the fuck now!"

He took out his cell phone and punched a speed dial. Pancho answered.

"Judi? What the hell is this about the CIA and FBI and DEA using some damned fishing boat to run a sting?"

"Oh. They are there?" Pancho replied. "Tell them to take a long walk on their pier. Maybe fade into the sunset. How's the weather there?"

"You know it's always like that! Fine! Better than usual! No, I won't look into it. Tell Marko he has the people here halfway around the world who can handle things better and faster than me."

"That's the story? Here and there or just there? My name's come up?"

"Yes. Both."

"The boys are right outside if you need help. Try to keep it down, okay? I don't want them exposed. They've worked very well in the past and I want to use them in the future."

"If you say so."

"So." Pancho giggled and dropped off. Clint

shook his head to keep from giggling himself.

"Well, it's a rumor she's sorry to have repeated. She never thought Mimi would even remember it. It doesn't concern me, but I might not be the one who would be concerned anyhow."

They looked uncomfortable. Inez was giving Hires looks that should leave scars! "I think I must take care of some business!" she snarled and walked out the door. Hires looked like he would faint.

"Have a good night!" Clint said. He and Judi went to a table. After a minute Hires went to the door and out. The two at the table looked at each other and left after dropping a twenty on the table. Ana came from the kitchen with a large tray with four specials on it.

"We'll take two of them here," Judi called. "It was nice of them to buy us dinner!"

Ana giggled.

"Do you think he has enough to keep him alive a week?" Judi asked.

"I think it's supposed to be in the states. If he was CIA, it was already released."

"In the states?"

"A man named Parks would be the one holding it, he would be the one running things. He had a heart attack and can't be reached."

They finished the meal and left. Clint went to

talk with Chico and tell what they'd done. In the morning Judi went back to Bocas Town. Clint would go to Santiago. He'd learned a thing or two. He hoped he could put an end to the real person behind this. Pancho had said something that made it likely it would start again.

Not if he had anything to say about it!

Santiago, win or lose, then home. He wanted to be with his wife and kids

Clint went to the steel grate gate to the big sprawling ranch house. The guard was a big man with a pony tail who had been described to him when this started.

"Clint Faraday. I have to speak with Carlos."

"You and a hundred others."

"Call him. Now, or I see you tagged for Gomez. Got it?"

"I don't know any Gomez. Take a hike!"

"Mariato. Video. You forcing him onto Hires' boat. Two witnesses. He didn't come back."

He suddenly didn't look so smug. He took out a little walky-talky and said should he let Clint Faraday in? He let Clint in.

Clint went to the door and a stern older woman said he was in back by the pool. He went around to find one of the men who was at the restaurant lounging there.

"Clint Faraday. I get a chance to be included in the conversation now?"

"We won't need an interpreter. Mimi is quite a character."

"What do you need to know, Mr. Faraday? –

And do you actually think I'll answer?"

"We have a video of your boy out there at the gate as much as carrying Gomez onto the boat. He didn't come back. Now Gomez has a brother looking for information about that trip and who was on it. You don't have protection from that bunch you put together anymore. They have to try to cover their own asses. They've discussed too much.

"Parks was a bad choice. Hires was worse. I doubt they really have a deal with the CIA, but everyone thinks they did now.

"They know about a lot of things, but they don't know you were really back of it. If they find that out, your ass is fertilizer."

"But you can't say I was behind anything. No one would believe you. I don't know where you got that idea. It is far from smart to suggest such things when you have no proof."

"I didn't suggest anything. There are people in the states who keep tabs on such things."

Selasia took a long drink from his glass and smirked at Clint.

"Marko is in the Mediterranean, Doniletti is in New York, Miklokaras is in Detroit. Jefferson is in Cleveland. No one is in California to learn anything. Don't spread rumors with no more than a hint or two from unspecified sources."

"You missed the one who's everywhere and has special interest in Central and South America. Parks actually had a heart attack when he learned you had that one's attention."

"I don't believe for a single second you know Mr. DeGulio, who is the only one who could bring about such a reaction by the mere mention of his name. Inez believed it and has become a problem to us. Others might, but I do not!"

Clint shook his head and took out his cell phone. He punched in a number from memory that very few people knew.

"Pancho? How are things?"

"Hello, Clint. What are you into now? Is there someone who must think I know?"

"Same old same old. Yes. Can I put you on speaker for you to explain the facts of life to Carlos Selasia? He doesn't believe his little scheme to consolidate crime here has caught your attention. It is to all of our advantages that he learns exactly how far this is going."

"Yes. Put him on." Clint put it on speaker. "He can see how he begins to annoy me with his petty little schemes. I do not enjoy my afternoons being interrupted with such shenanigans."

"You're on. How is the wife and son?"

"We are well and happier than anyone has a right to be, Clint. I think I will come to visit you on the comarca. I will like the place, as Dave and Judi and others have.

"Is Judi there?"

"No. I am in Santiago with Selasia. He's living in some fantasy world where he makes a shit to anything. He thinks he can continue with his stupid plot to take over crime in the Americas."

"He only thinks he can think.

"Mr. Selasia, you will retire as of today. You have made enough to live a long and pleasant life. Should you decide to not follow this friendly fatherly advice you will not have a long – and very certainly not a pleasant life. Those you involved to this point are trying to find a way to escape the stupidity of speaking of various matter with anyone, much less people such as themselves. The only safety is for the last survivor,which assumes there will be no new faces in the interim. How you deal with them is your affair. I wish to have no further involvement in such sordid actions. I hope that is made clear enough for even such as you to understand?"

Selasia was sweating, but was determined to brave it out. "It would be if you were actually Mr. DeGulio. I don't believe that!

"I know! I know your real name! What is it?"

"Francisco Veras DeGulio Vila."

"Oh, god!"

"Am I clear enough *now*, Sr. Selasia?"

"Yes, Sir! I'm sorry, Sir!"

"Then we need not speak further of this."

"No, Sir. I do have enough to live on. I just wanted to see if I could do it."

"Many others want to see if they can do it. They all go about it the wrong way. One gains respect, which is power, by how he conducts himself. You may inspire fear, as is your wont, but that is not respect. You will get a facade of respect, but it is not that and you know it. You earn respect by what you do for people, not what you do to them.

"Clint, Inez, who you met, is trying to make a deal with two others. That deal concerns Mr. Selasia. I think you can figure his long life is no part of their plans. There is already a plot among two of the plotters to overthrow her if she is successful.

"It begins. They will kill each other off.

"Mr. Selasia, I would suggest you not leave your secure premises nor allow any of the people you thought were working with you in for about three months. It should be over by then to the extent it ever will be.

"Clint, I really do think I will visit you one day. I have never met your wife and children. I wish to do so. I have reports that your son, in particular, is quite the outspoken major intelligence on the comarca."

"Everyone but myself and he thinks he's a genius. He's smart, but I doubt he's a genius."

They chatted a minute more, then Clint rang off and said he would be going. Be careful even of those he thought he could trust. They were standing at the door. The gateman was lolling against the post.

"I agree. I will go to a place I know is safe for a few months."

Clint went to the station and got the next bus to David. He would get his car there and soon be home!

He wondered if Selasia would live out the month. He wondered how many of the schemers would be alive in Pancho's three months.

Not many. The ones who survived would have an extra incentive to look over their shoulders the rest of their lives.

What a way to live!

If you could call that living.

Clint held onto Tyna for a long moment. Nito and Nicole hung onto them.

"It's so good to be home again! I thought this would be the one that cures me of the detective thing, but we both know I'll be running off again. I'll try to make it things that are more puzzles than this kind of violent stupidity.

"I talked with Pancho DeGulio, who Dave talks about a lot. Nick and Janet are friends. He might come to visit."

The chopper pilot waved and rose. Clint and family headed for the house.

"Anything happen while I was gone?"

"Well, Kiki Caldez seduced your son. He's learning why we like to spend so much time in bed I think," Tyna answered. "Basilio said the business you and Manny set up with that man on Popa is doing so well others are petitioning Manny to finance the same thing for them.

"Matilde says Jada's pregnant and will have a girl she names Rubia. Omar found a new place for lobster he won't tell anyone about because they'll fish it out too fast.

"That's from Cusapín, of course. Nito getting laid was here.

"Dave and Alma are in Darien and won't be back for weeks if not months. Sergio called and said he had to solve a murder all by himself and used your methods. Judi helped.

"Judi told me about what she did in Mariato. She likes being an airhead.

"Things are, as you can see, normal. For us!"

Clint held her again. Nito said, "Time for all that sex stuff! Let's go to the stream."

"Might as well," Nicole replied.

www.ingramcontent.com/pod-product-compliance
Lightning Source LLC
Chambersburg PA
CBHW050610160726
48003CB00003B/1125